BÊTE NOIRE

FEAR IS JUST A POINT OF VIEW

Editors:

A. W. Gifford

Jennifer L. Gifford

P.O. Box 811
Ortonville, MI 48462

www.betenoiremagazine.com

Bête Noire is published by Dark Opus Press a division of Charm Noir Omnimedia P.O Box 1545, Highland, MI 48357

ISBN: 978-0692294628

In This Issue

The Devils of Somerset, Mississippi – Jeremy Lloyd Beck   1

Backseat Driver – Luke Spooner   12

Bristlecone – James Frederick William Rowe   13

Transient Number Five – Christian Riley   16

Shot Down #225 – Eleanor Leonne Bennett   19

Rock On – Marge Simon   20

2 – Wojciech Zwolinski   22

The Art of Becoming – J. J. Steinfeld   23

Eyes of the Dog – Tobacco Jones   25

Group – Luke Spooner   36

The House – Carol Hornak   37

The Last Promise – Denny E. Marshall   39

Blood Debt – JD Cano   40

The Devils of Somerset, Mississippi

Jeremy Lloyd Beck

I saw it at thirty thousand feet: the schools and roads, the rows of houses, the big Baptist church. It was the secret face of Somerset, Mississippi, the one you don't see in the brochures. An entire town laid out as a giant pentagram.

I'm not superstitious. A shape's a shape, but in a world of superstition it makes sense that the rent is cheap.

The town's been like that for years, one development at a time, a new street or school, a new church steeple, then a pentagram. Nobody noticed until the advent of commercial flight when – like me, now – a little face pushed against airplane glass and saw the mark of Satan etched into the face of Mississippi.

"Startles most folks that fly in. Ain't nothing to worry about," my new landlord said. He was a southern gentleman with two months' rent and a Jesus fish on his t-shirt. "'Specially safe here." He smiled, chuckling, jumbling my lease and his keys in his hands.

I called my new home the Shakespeare house because it was on Shakespeare street, just down from the Baptist church.

"You know, a lot of them live in this building too," he said, "the interns are upstairs, one of the old office gals is in the room on the end. Are you baptist?"

"Atheist," I replied, squeezing my new key onto it's ring, looking up in time to catch a handful of disappointment and awkward silence before he finally left.

"Well, there's a lot of God here in Somerset."

"Believe me," I said, "there's really not."

I came to Somerset to get away from home. I picked it because they needed an English teacher and were willing to pay extra. There was only one public school in Somerset—most of the kids were put in prep schools attached to one church or another. I was warned that I might get *the rough kids,* but they meant the black ones. The AP English teacher had a white—washed classroom full of kids who could barely read.

And they didn't need to; after all, the Bible is on iTunes these days.

Thanks to iTunes, these kids will learn about their God, but, by semester's end, know nothing more of themselves, their country, their devils. What good is learning about God and forgetting the Devil?

Set in colonial Boston, The Devil and Tom Walker is one of the earliest short stories in American history. Written by Washington Irving, who also—and more famously—wrote the Legend of Rip Van Winkle. Although the Devil and Tom Walker is strongly influenced by Goethe's *Faust,* Irving reinvents the tale into something quintessentially American, he makes it a necessary part of the American canon, *the American Bible.*

It is not on iTunes.

"Mister *Apples,*" a pretty little blue—eyed girl in the front began.

"Ap*pels.* Not the fruit."

"Mister *Appeeellllsss,*" she corrected, lips and accent stretching around the words like rubber. "My daddy said I shouldn't read stories like that."

"Like what?"

"Like about Satan and witchcraft. He said it's just inviting the evil," she said. "That's why good Christians don't read *Twilight.*"

"The Devil and Tom Walker is an American classic. It's not evil."

"The Devil ain't evil?" Another said. "Shoot... Where you go to church, mister *Apples?*"

"While we can certainly see religious influence on the piece, this isn't a religious piece. This is not a story about the Christian devil, not so much as it's about an American sense of fear, even perhaps American Deism."

"Mister *Apples?*"

"You see, it's not just about Tom Walker's deal with the devil, but there's something else going on here too. Anybody?" I glanced around the silent room. "It's not just about the concern that the devil is among us — something most of you may feel — but there's something else very sneaky happening in the text. Name?" I pointed.

"J — Jonah."

"Where's God in the Devil and Tom Walker?"

"I d — didn't read."

"Well, where do you say God is?"

"Heaven?"

"Then you, like Tom Walker, certainly didn't find him in early American Boston."

"'Cause of all the liberals?"

Somerset revolved around a little Baptist church down the street from the Shakespeare house. Every weekend was a potluck or a bake sale, always at the church, always packed out the street, and always, *always*, food.

No wonder baptists seem so engorged.

Every weekend was an experiment in roadway congestion as half the town poured themselves into my front yard to wait in line for the weekend's event. Last week, the car show; this week, the *Molasses Festival*.

"You should come, Dennis," the *other* English teacher prodded. "It's a Somerset tradition." Before I could decline, he reached out and gave my elbow a squeeze, added, "you could even try your luck in the picnic auction."

He winked; I hated when people did that.

"Do you have those up North?"

I'm from Florida.

"You bid on a picnic basket and the highest bidder goes out with the girl who made it," he smiled, his gray eyebrows splayed in all directions. "That's how I met missus King, you know."

"But then I couldn't be single."

"Oh ho! You are a riot."

The Shakespeare house — a cramped flat *slash* roomy coffin — wasn't much to look at, and even less to be in. The kitchen sink was full of rust. The bathroom floors were tiled in mismatched and crooked layers: you could see three or four different patterns deep in spots, where *un*-handyman after *un*-handyman had neatly matched the skewed tiles on top of each other. Several of the kitchen cabinet doors were different colors from being replaced; all the shelf liners were different. It was an electric fire waiting to happen.

The classic philosophers debated about a ship from Athens whose parts had all been replaced—one by one—over the years after its maiden voyage. They wondered if the Athenian ship could - after its many repairs—still be called the same ship. Though far from the cultured forums of Athens, the Shakespeare house was certainly an *Athenian apartment*—a building built and rebuilt, probably since the dawn of time.

Imagine cave men huddled in the *Shakespeare lean – to.*

And if that didn't sell you, my next door neighbor Catherine—a sweet girl and probable meth cook—told me that when she was little the apartments were rented mostly to prostitutes.

"We used to call it red—light alley," she said between puffs on her cigarette, "because they all changed out their porch lights."

Like traffic lights for the perverse, red means go at the Shakespeare house.

"We egged the place sometimes, never thought I'd live here." She was probably twenty—five, her teeth were stained with tobacco and whitening strips. While talking, she occasionally slipped her hand under her shirt to scratch her midriff.

"Why stay?"

"It's cheap. You know that."

"In Somerset?"

"Hell if I know," she said, flicking her ashes to the ground, squishing the glowing ones underfoot. "Everyone stays."

That weekend, I walked through my squeaking door, past Catherine the meth cook's room, and down to the baptist church and the surrounding sprawl of tables, booths, and dunk tanks. Food carts full of treats peppered the streets. Sticky children and big—haired Baptist mothers gossiped about their neighbors and husbands. The trees were decorated with little burlap dolls, stained with molasses, hung by their necks.

Tables with picnic baskets lined the sidewalk. At the end of the row, a wrinkled woman takes the bids for the auction. In a minute, an old Baptist preacher will walk out the front doors of the church and announce the results and he'll do it in full black face. Catherine told me he did it every year.

"What is this supposed to commemorate?"

"Molasses, sugar," the homely lady – done up like Aunt Jemima – said. "What else?"

"Well," I began, "the decorations seem to be a touch. . ."

"Spit it out now, darlin'. Ain't got all day."

"Do they pay you to dress like that?"

"Why every year!" She beamed. "What about the decorations is botherin' you now?"

"They look like... Was there a division of the Klan in Somerset?"

Shock, offense, a spoonful of outrage.

"You tryin' to take an innocent, sweet holiday and turn it into something evil now, ain't you?" She slapped my arm, I shrunk back. "Is that what you teachin' my grandbabies in that school? Prejudice, mister *Apples*?"

She slapped me again before Mr. King—the racist English teacher—pulled me away.

"Oh, miss Maisie, let me steal mister *Apples* from you for a moment," he said, grabbing my arm. "And put fifty dollars down on lot 16 for me, would you kindly?"

"You can take him to the city limits and dump him out for all I care! Devil take him!" She spat on the ground as he pulled me away.

"You got to be careful around Maisie's likes, mister *Apples*," he said, sweet—tongue bending around the words like a serpent. "What you say to get her so riled?"

"It's this festival...It's..." I didn't know how to say it to someone like King.

"Oh don't be so sensitive! It isn't like that." He smiled, patted my back. "Why up North you all pay so much attention to those sort of things. Here we've learned not to take things so seriously. It just works better. Now I hope your hungry, 'cause you're going to win lot 16 over there."

"I don't want to bid on anything."

"You're not biddin' on anybody, Dennis. I'm biddin' on you," he said. "You see over there?"

Mr. King points to a group of girls my age, with sweet smiles and deceptive eyes. Catherine circled the edge, barred clenched teeth through an ineffective smile, bound in a Sunday dress.

"My daughter hates these things but I make her come anyway." He smiled at me, cupped my neck. "Do me a favor? Make it easier for her."

I nodded and, as Catherine predicted, the pastor comes out in black face, led by the mayor and a deacon.

"Look! Pastor Lucas's a negro for the day!" Big miss Maisie squealed. "Look everybody! It's *Passa!*"

⋙✠⋘

When I met her, I didn't know her name was Catherine *King*. When I asked about it, she treated it like a dark secret, like a deformation or the uncle you lock in the basement when company's over. Mrs. King made the basket for her and daddy made her go along with it or he'd stop paying her rent. We spent that evening behind the church, on the top level of a jungle gym where nobody could see her smoking. She left her butts tucked in a corner.

"You really don't see it? You don't see the little *Sambo* puppets in the trees?"

"It's not that I don't see them, I just don't care," she said, smoke puffing out with her words. A long drag. "It's tradition, not a statement."

"It's permission," I said. "It's a gold stamp on every lynching that happened here. It's not evil: it's performance art, social commentary."

"And what is it commenting?"

"Jesus was Aryan and crucify all else."

"Bible truth." She laughed like a dragon, smoke billowing, eyes red. Dead air kills.

"Didn't peg you for a church—type."

"Give 'em long enough, everyone in Somerset is a church—type." She nodded her head to me as she balanced her next cigarette in between her lips. "You think you're not, gossip says you're not, but you're here."

"Someone else paid for it."

"And it tasted like ass." She said. "You get what you pay for."

"I'm not a church—type." A dozen couples sat on the church lawn, I recognized half the buyers as married men. "It's empty. Hollow halls is more like it."

She didn't reply, just puffed away, made me end the silence.

I asked, "Do I at least get a free smoke with the meal?"

"My specialty." She passed me her half—empty carton. "You'll go all the same, too tempting not to."

"You go then?"

"Course not. But I will. Just give me time and lung cancer and I'll be in the front row. You really smoke?"

"One time. Didn't like it."

"Why now?"

"Seemed like the thing to do."

"Sounds like you'll be right next to me yet, you'll see."

"You'll be wearing the frumpy head scarf?"

"Singing the Grace Amazing 'til God fails my malignant little corpse."

We smoked into the night until it got dark and a deacon saw the light of our cigarettes. He demanded that we put them out and leave. We did both, but we didn't stop at the Shakespeare house.

"Want to get wasted?" I asked.

"No liquor on the weekends."

"That's dumb."

"Mayor doesn't want anybody hungover during church." She turned to me and squinted. "You mean that earlier? About the festival being evil?"

"Why wouldn't I?"

"I didn't think you guys believed in evil," she said. "You know, atheists."

"Does everyone know that?"

"Word gets around."

"Of course I believe in evil. No demons or anything like that, but lots of things are evil. I don't need a pompous sky man to tell me killing babies is evil. Some things stick out."

"But its got to come from somewhere."

I stopped.

"Here's the thing: For you, you get cancer. You suck it up during chemo—radiation—your guts turn to jelly. You can't walk, talk, that lovely dinner we just had tastes like a handful of nickels and makes you vomit all over the floor. You do one of two things: you have your family drag your shrunken ass to church, and hope that the God that caused it will lift his smiting fingers from you; or you blame the cancer sticks you huffed on the jungle gym. It's not about gods or monsters, it's about responsibility; who gets the blame? Who's the ultimate asshole?"

"You really aren't the church—type."

"No kidding?"

"I'm heading back."

"Don't blame you."

"See you 'round?"

"Probably."

She left, turned around and walked off. She carried her shoes in one hand, flicked her ashes away with the other. For a second, I stared at her ass.

It was dark, pitch black night and I'd passed all the streetlamps by –
they only reached a few hundred feet past the Shakespeare house. I
passed the deli, the old fashioned ice cream shop, the gas station
where *Gomer Pyle* got his start: it was the American Dream, or, maybe,
the dream America. Somerset looked the part.

In the distance, I saw the oak that marked the edge of town – the
edge of all the insanity. I thought about crossing it, just walking
straight out of Somerset and all the way back to Florida, a failure but
still sane, defeated but not broken. I laughed it off, thought about a
half—bottle of vodka in my fridge. I thought, *maybe Catherine would go
for a nightcap?*

Under the tree, I saw the whispers of a glow, just a small one, a meager burst of flame in the night. Then another, a handful of flickers.

I could see them now, hanging from the tree. *The burlap black folk?* I
wondered if molasses burned. *Enough sugar I suppose.* A prank? Do I
call the fire department? I wanted to see up close.

At the great tree at the edge of town, I stopped to look at the pretty
little fires, but they weren't little burlap men. I reached up with my
jacket around my hands and patted until the fire stopped. A man in
the shadows hoisted his debris into the trees and in my fingers a
burned and severed hand. In the man's hand is a rope, thrown over a
bough; in his other, *miss Maisie's head.*

"What is this?" I heaved.

It was little burning bits, bits of miss Maisie.

The head sprung to flame and swung into the air, released from its
dark master's hand. He turned. In his black robes and darkened hood,
I could feel him smile.

"Why aren't you in bed for church?"

"Atheist," I whispered.

He pulled a dagger from his flowing robes and held it to the light,
the tip glistened with blood and poison. A forked tongue slithered
from under his hood and wrapped the blade, drinking it in.

"What are you doing?" I asked stupidly. I tried to stop, but *I kept going.*

He turned back to me, stalked me.

"Back off." My hand raised to challenge him.

He kept coming.

"Stop."

His dagger glowed in the firelight.

I couldn't move.

"Please."

He pulled back his hand, his blade.

My legs took control of my mind and I ran. I ran down the street, past the gas station, the old fashioned ice cream shop, the deli. I saw the glinting knife and a serene grin, like nirvana, reflected in the storefronts around me. I ran and ran and didn't look back. I ran until I was where Catherine left, then I kept running. I ran until the Shakespeare house.

I *should* have kept going.

I stopped to catch my breath and looked over my shoulder: there he was, walking—gliding—gently down main street toward me.

I passed the first apartment, and the second.

I was fast, but still he swept toward me, right down the street. I pulled out my keys as I went. He was at the curb.

My hand shook as I slid my key into the lock. He was on the sidewalk.

The door opened itself. Another man of shadow stood inside, waiting. I felt his smile.

I pulled backwards as he reached, his black hand drifting – like a breaststroke – toward me. The dagger thrust toward me from my side. The doors, I saw them, covered in blood – all but mine. A third on the second floor, on the balcony. He climbed over the rail and floated gently to the ground.

"Dennis?" I heard Catherine ask in the dark, from opened door. The specters turning to her for a second as she glanced around—blindly. She shrugged and closed her door.

We were alone again.

I stepped back; turned to run, the monster on my heel.

Cornered, I went in the only direction I could. I found myself running to the church. *That's supposed to stop them, right?* I thought, too busy running to fight it. *The devil can't follow me there.*

Three of them now.

Over my shoulder I felt the second and third brandish their weapons. I ran down the lawn, I passed the dunk tank and the little burlap men in the trees, their little hand—stitched mouths wide open, laughing, singing.

"Where will you run?" They sang. "Where will you hide?"

I reached the steps and my foot slipped on the first step. My head hit the concrete and for a moment it was all black, then a peek of the three dark men fanning out around me, a peek of my blood on the step. I wiped my forehead and felt a gash, blood and loose tissue oozing out like jelly donuts.

The molasses men sang: "Where can you go that the devil can't find?"

I pushed my hand down. The world turned violently. Gravity bore upwards. Everything pulled to the left. Up, I climbed the step and dug my legs uselessly at the ground until one finally caught the ground. I pushed and pulled and pleaded myself forward another inch – then two – as the men in black slid toward me. I kept writhing, kept fighting my way up the steps and I reached for the door.

I yelled.

The devil behind me slid his blade – the very tip in my calf – down my leg. I kicked back with the other until I was free and upright. Falling to the door, I grabbed the handle, twisting, tugging, forcing it open. I limped inside.

Sanctuary.

But I kept going.

My feet stumbled forward—not limping or hobbling. I looked down at the trail of blood I left in the aisle. Tripping, reached out for a pew, steadied myself on my way to the altar. I looked over my shoulder at the demons watching from the door and grabbed a Bible from the back of the pew, held like a shield.

"Suck on it," I yelled, pushing off the pew, stumbled backward to the altar at the front of the church.

I expected to hit the stage, but I kept going—*everything pulled to the left.*

And I cringed.

I cringed as I pulled the tablecloth and sacrament trays off the altar. I cringed as I saw my pursuers cross the threshold. And I cringed when a final wraith stopped my fall and when his dagger hit my kidney.

He let me roll off the blade to the ground. On my back, I held up the Bible as they gathered around. I turned it over in my hands and opened the pages.

All blank.

I dropped the book and finally saw him. The one who stabbed me, his shroud lowered, I saw *Passa.* I pulled myself back, to the steps of the stage, back and up. They closed in around me: Pastor Lucas, the mayor, my landlord, *Mr. King.*

"Do atheists believe in devils, Dennis?" My landlord whispered.

"You don't believe in no devils, do you now?" Mr. King asked.

"Help!" I yelled, crawling to the back of the sanctuary, to the crucifix behind the pulpit.

The mayor smiled.

I crawled, and I cried, and I reached to the cross. But I never felt God. Only the blades. Only the words. I cried for salvation, and nobody heard me, nobody but the devils of Somerset, Mississippi.

Jeremy Lloyd Beck *is a writer and teacher in Georgia. Though his award–winning short films have appeared in several festivals, The Devils of Somerset, Mississippi is his first magazine publication.*

BACKSEAT DRIVER *by Luke Spooner*

Luke Spooner *a.k.a. 'Carrion House' currently lives and works in the South of England. Having recently graduated from the University of Portsmouth with a first class degree he is now a full time illustrator for just about any project that peaks his interest. Despite regular forays into children's books and fairy tales his true love lies in anything macabre, melancholy or dark in nature and essence. He believes that the job of putting someone else's words into a visual form, to accompany and support their text, is a massive responsibility as well as being something he truly treasures.*

www.carrionhouse.com
www.facebook.com/carrionhouse

BRISTLECONE

James Frederick William Rowe

You may know my age, but you know me not
Neither do you know yourselves
Only I know you, for I know what you were
Before you were as you are now

King Disor's own daughter planted me
In this, which was once his mountain garden
Knowing that I would endure the ages
She named me Nmrtijos - immortal

You have named me Methuselah
A good a name as any you could concoct
Indeed, better than you realize
As I knew the world that was

For a century I was the prize of the garden
Living testament to Disor's divine reign
His life, like mine, seeming without end
But even Gods taste of death

The war was fought in a single battle
All from afar: From across the oceans
Between continents, through the air
Bolts of the fire of hell and light of the sun

Thousands filled the sky
And thousands more met them
Their fury stained the sky
Their power broke the Earth

Silence followed the din
A silence unnatural in its depth
Evil in its totality
The sun rose on a dead world, cloaked in smoke

For a thousand years was I alone
But eventually they came again
When I saw their red skin
I thought them still burnt from the blasts

They, like you, were a mere remnant
Survivors in savagery from the war
And the winter which froze the seas
And the summer which flooded the land

I saw in their faces an insult
To the dignity of the mighty of old
But also hope for the future
That one day you may again be great

So did I watch your progress
And was told by the wind
Of the civilization you built
In ignorance of that which came before

I learned that in legend
You dimly recollected your past
But Atlantis is an empty word
Shangrilla merely a dream

Neverthless, you grew in power
And as the aeons passed, in pride
Not yet like Disor, not yet divine
But near enough, near enough

Then one day I saw it
The same fire, the same light
Just one and far away
Not yet a calamity - but the promise of one

So now I wait to see how long it shall be
Till the cycle of history resets
When will the skies ignite again?
When will the poison snow fall once more?

When you are destroyed I will remain
I will persist, though you will not
And I shall remember you as I have the others
When you are but legends for those who shall come

James Frederick William Rowe *is a Rhysling-nominated poet and author out of Brooklyn, New York. In the last few years, he has cut out a substantial niche in the speculative poetry front, having seen over twenty-five poems published internationally in such markets as* Big Pulp, Songs of Eretz, Tale of the Talisman, Heroic Fantasy Quarterly, Andromeda Spaceways In-flight Magazine, *and now* Bete Noire. *When he is not writing verses and crafting yarns, he is employed as an adjunct professor of philosophy in the City University of New York, is pursuing a Ph.D. in the same subject, and works a variety of freelance positions.*

Bristlecone *is dedicated to Whittney, whose mind-blowing distress at the mere mention of ancient nuclear conflict inspired the poem. Further, the poet's website can be found at http://jamesfwrowe.wordpress.com*

Transient Number Five

Christian Riley

I held a brother in my arms this night—every last piece of him—then I took him down to the cold water of Higgins Lake and threw him far and wide. A fathom plus should be enough to smother his grief. Not that it matters any, but it's the thought that counts. Besides, all that lonely, muddy darkness will sure make for one hell of a grave.

I never did get my brother's name. I only knew him as Transient Number Five. He had his piece of the American Dream, a two-foot wide concrete divider at the corner of 5th and Watt. That's where I'd see him pass his hours in silent seclusion from society. His voice was the mundane plea for help scribbled onto a flap of cardboard, seen at just about every busy intersection in town. But he was my brother, and I knew his thoughts, which were anything but the ordinary, commonplace burdens of a civilized world. My brother never really cared about being out of gas, or out of money, homeless and desperate and in dying need of a shower and a hot meal. And he sure as hell didn't care about being out of work. All that mattered at the end of the day was a 5th of Jack Daniel's and an overpass.

Like I said, I knew my brother's thoughts, and they were anything but mundane. Quite the opposite, they were spectacular! Brilliant and burning, filled with the kind of exclamatory bliss found only in watching the land turn red from your enemy's eviscerated entrails.

So why his long face? Why his sluggish and decayed deeds, his crumbling visage, his complete and utter depletion of hope?

Back in the day, the long, long day, a brother was never in want of an overpass to hide his shame. Such shame simply did not exist. Transient Number Five, and men like him, men like me, once stood as haughty creatures. We once swaggered onto shiny battlefields, our swords swinging through grisly gore, our arrogant grins exposing pearly teeth as pinkish mist and chunked bone arced high into a leaden sky. Even as late as the Great War, Number Five would have known his place — in a tank, perhaps — amidst the sounds of twisting steel, and screaming men, with the smell of burning powder and burning flesh, but this man, this man of stone, would have undoubtedly kept a lazy smile on his face throughout it all. For nothing can conquer a man who dies with a purpose.

And at the end of those long days, rest assured there was liquor; pints and gallons, amidst the sounds of laughter and tears. There were the smells of victory, and of women. There was the soft touch of flesh, the embracement of love, and the sweet whisper that gave a man his reasons to live, to die. His purpose.

This evening I took a drive. I picked up dinner, turned on Albion Street then hit the corner of 5th and Watt. I saw my brother standing there, and everything about him told me that he was finished. All that was missing was a salute, as he stood at attention, tall and powerful. No more slumped shoulders, bent knees, craned neck and long face with a thousand-yard stare fixed at a pebble on the ground. Transient Number Five had found a place once again, I'd realized, amidst our pitiless society.

I pulled into a parking lot that gave me a good view of the man, and then I chuckled; he was holding his sign upside down. The humor was short-lived however, as I knew that moments like this almost never ended well. As if on cue, a dark cloud rolled in, releasing random droplets at first, and then a volley of hail ending with a steady deluge. Nevertheless, Transient Number Five held fast at his corner, and the hours passed.

At about the time my ass was killing me, my brother made a quick about-face then filed ahead, marching with the kind of deliberate fervor seen prior to "the battle." He released his grip on the scrap of cardboard and I watched it drift down into a puddle.

Here it comes, I thought, slipping out of my car in careful succession. I was torn like an athlete's ACL, one half fearing for my brother, wanting to run up and tell him to cool down, that I felt his pain, that there were others like him; and the other half that just said *fuck it*. Fuck it, *because* of the pain, and all the others. And fuck it because of the thankless nods from a society too dumb to realize what was missing.

Transient Number Five forged ahead with his newfound purpose. Slinking in the shadows, I caught a glimpse of his profile as he passed under an old street lamp. His face looked like aged granite, stolid and weathered, and I had the fleeting impression that this man couldn't smile now even if he wanted to. Nor could he frown.

He left a trail of gray sludge that had me thinking of irritable smoke chained to the wet ground, asphyxiated and writhing with torment for its release. Easy to follow now, I fell back biding my time. I was more curious and less anxious, as he was heading for the outskirts of town. Past the rundown lumber mill and across from Spencer's Tack and Feed, Transient Number Five stopped at the base of a small embankment. He cocked an ear to the south, and I think I heard it just about the same time he did—the train whistle.

In the end, I sided with "Fuck it." I picked a good tree to lean against, and watched as my brother decidedly climbed that embankment. At the top, he took in a lungful of air then positioned himself in the center of the tracks, standing at attention. And this time, he did salute.

It was the northbound Greyhound, clocking at about sixty miles an hour. Transient Number Five exploded into an array of concrete shrapnel and dust, and thus ended the tour of my brother, fellow warrior, man of stone.

Hours later, on my way back to my car, I crossed paths with that scrap of cardboard—Number Five's final words. It was soggy as a wet tortilla, but legible all the same. Nothing mundane of course—out of money, gas, or work—it simply reads "out of love," and the irony draws a pensive smile to my face even now. His purpose, my purpose, *our* purpose...all done out of love.

Christian Riley's stories have appeared in over sixty magazines and anthologies, across various genres. As a previous citizen of the Pacific Northwest, he vows one day to return, knowing that that which has yet to be discovered lurks somewhere behind the Redwood Curtain. He keeps a static blog of his writings at frombehindthebluedoor.wordpress.com, and can be reached at chakalives@gmail.com.

SHOT DOWN 225 *by Eleanor Leonne Bennett*

❧✠☙

Eleanor Leonne Bennett *is an eighteen-year-old internationally award win-ning photographer and artist who has won first places with* National Geographic, The World Photography Organization, Nature's Best Photography, Papworth Trust, Mencap, The Woodland Trust *and* Postal Heritage. *Her photography has been published in the* Telegraph, The Guardian, BBC News Website *and on the cover of books and magazines in the United states and Canada. Her art is also globally exhibited.*

Rock On

Marge Simon

It happens
in this day and age
you can't tell
life from virtual.

His said his parents owed him
like all parents owe their kids
a matter of rights (his)
a matter of wrongs (theirs)
so he was just showing them all
how good he was

as star of a reality show
that got a little too real
something the girl whispered
with her hand on his joy stick
his tongue in her ear

that caused his fingers
to curl around her neck,
made them squeeze
until the camera went dark,
millions watching.

In the final segment,
so young, so dumb, so full of mirth,
a sunbeam floods the scaffold;
twelve steps to the top, high noon
until the hood falls.

But it's not a hangman's rope,
it's an oak chair,
He's belted in tight,
screaming at the folks
behind the camera
until some guy in blue
presses the button.

That part was real,
the stench of burning hair.

He wanted fame,
wanted what was owed him.
He got it.

Rock on.

Marge Simon's *works appear in publications such as* Strange Horizons, Niteblade, DailySF Magazine, Pedestal Magazine, Dreams & Nightmares. *She edits a column for the HWA Newsletter and serves as Chair of the Board of Trustees. She has won the Strange Horizons Readers Choice Award, the Bram Stoker Award™(2008, 2012, 2013), the Rhysling Award and the Dwarf Stars Award. Collections:* Like Birds in the Rain, Unearthly Delights, The Mad Hattery, Vampires, Zombies & Wanton Souls, *and* Dangerous Dreams. Member HWA, SFWA, SFPA. *www.margesimon.com*

Ƶ by Wojciech Zwolinski

Born in 1986, Wojciech's *been a photographer since 2006, though it was just a hobby at first. He took his first step in serious artistic education in 2007 and discovered that photography is his biggest passion.*

He studied at National Higher School of Film, Television and Theatre in Łódź (Poland) and graduated in 2014. He is working as a freelancer with various people, from writers to fashion designers and as a contributing photographer, sharing his photos with photo libraries.

He's interested mainly in dark art, gothic, industrial, alternative fashion and also in fantasy of all sorts.

The Art of Becoming In-Visible

J. J. Steinfeld

Why doesn't anyone answer
my well composed inquiries
sent at every solstice, equinox,
and partial or full eclipse,
punctually year after year?

Why doesn't anyone answer
my succinct yet solemn prayers
when cacophony is approaching myth
periodically here and there?

Why doesn't anyone see
my impressive touching of the moon
during less than desirable nights
haphazardly once in awhile?

And why does that figure with the gun
yell at me to turn around
just as I've mastered
the art of becoming invisible?

CB✠BO

Canadian poet, fiction writer, and playwright J. J. Steinfeld *lives on Prince Edward Island, where he is patiently waiting for Godot's arrival and a phone call from Kafka. While waiting, he has published fourteen books, including* **Should the Word Hell Be Capitalized?** *(Stories, Gaspereau Press),* **Would You Hide Me?** *(Stories, Gaspereau Press),* **An Affection for Precipices** *(Poetry, Serengeti Press),* **Misshapenness** *(Poetry, Ekstasis Editions),* **Word Burials** *(Novel and Stories, Crossing Chaos Enigmatic Ink), and* **A Glass Shard and Memory** *(Stories, Recliner Books). More than three hundred of his short stories and nearly six hundred poems have appeared in anthologies and periodicals internationally, and over forty of his one-act plays and a handful of full-length plays have been performed in Canada and the United States.*

EYES OF THE DOG

Tobacco Jones

1. Mom

"Don't leave," said the girl, just like she did every day. "Stay with us today, please mama?"

The boy felt the same, but at the age of nine he had become cynical. He said nothing as Mom strapped him in to his TV chair.

Mom was fighting back tears and panic, just like she did every day when the nanny didn't show up.

"DeeDee will be here soon, my loves," Mom cooed. "I'm leaving you some special foodpaks today: veggie-ham-pineapple mix and powdered candycake."

The boy said nothing.

"Foodpaks are too sweet," said the girl.

"It's not real sugar," said Mom, wondering how any child could find something too sweet. "Don't worry."

"Can't we have real food, like we used to?" said the girl.

"People kept getting fat," said Mom. "So they made it illegal. We can't buy it anymore."

Mom looked up at one of the microcams, hating it, wishing too for the real food.

"I've got to go now, pumpkins," said Mom, giving them each a hug and a kiss and turning on the TV on her way out.

Mom got into her boxcar and hummed out of their small driveway, round and round and back and forth and then out of the superdivision. She was lucky to live here, she thought. She feared the day would come that they would knock down the superdivision and put in a hive, like they were doing everywhere. "I don't want my kids living in a hive," she said out loud, not even caring if the boxcar microcams picked it up.

Mom merged onto the greenway, her boxcar zipping into the raildrive and attaching itself into the train. Snaking her way into the big city, Mom thought about the kids and crossed her fingers DeeDee would be there soon. Mom wondered why the actuaries union made her work six ten-hour days every week, while the nannies union let DeeDee show up whenever.

Mom had complained once, to the union like you are supposed to. Got her hand slapped, bad. Convicted of some isms, she got a ten percent tax hike on top of the ninety-two she was already paying, this putting her a couple points into the negative. Nearly wiped out her savings before they reduced the sentence to five points, but the wealth tax that year took the rest.

Now Mom had been working hard for the better part of two years and had saved up twenty nanogolds, enough to buy her kids presents for Allholiday. She passed ChildMart every day, always wanting to detach and stop in. Then she would be at the counter with a toy car and a doll, and the price would be twenty nanogolds, including all taxes, and she would have just enough on her G-card and she would pay for the toys and take them in a ChildMart bag out to her boxcar and put them in the trunk, and she would smile all the way home.

2. Girl

The girl cried and cried, just like she did every day after Mom left, whether DeeDee was there or not. Her brother glared at her from his strapchair, turning his head like an owl.

There was no children's programming on the government channel. Mom said this was cause kids were supposed to live in Orphies, not home watching GTV, but Mom was stubborn and kept her kids. And even though they didn't know any other kids, and they only got learning from Mom on Sundays, and even though DeeDee was not there sometimes, the girl was happy that Mom had kept her.

The girl saw an Orphie on TV once, the biggest place she had ever seen. Millions of kids lined up across the sports fields to spell out the name of the place, *MidWest Regional Child Development Center No. 243, the Redhawks.* The TV man said they had been practicing this all year. Said you could see it from space. The girl still didn't want to go there.

Today's TV programming was some math people talking about technology something offset productivity decline something farming. The girl wondered if that was the sort of math Mom did.

"We've got rid of the last private farms," said some drawly pundit. "Problem oughtta be licked."

"Replacing workers with machines is the only way," said some other guy.

"Afraid so," said the first guy. "People these day just don't understand what hard work is about. They talk a good game, but in the end it's always what's in it for them."

The girl got an itch, then, someplace on her back that she could usually reach but the straps were wide across her arms and chest, so she could barely reach her own shoulders. She struggled for a while, then gave up, trying to make friends with the itch instead of fighting it.

Her brother swiveled his head again. "Gotta pee?" he said. "Better hold it."

A couple of times when DeeDee had not shown up at all, the girl had peed her strapchair. She was scared Mom would be angry but she was stuck so she just sat in the pee and hoped it would go away and not smell too bad and Mom wouldn't notice. But Mom did notice and she wasn't mad and she cleaned it up, but not before getting the girl into the tub and clean and then tucked into bed with an extra squirtberry foodpak. The girl thought she saw tears in Mom's eyes, then, but it was hard to tell through her own tears, so she got in bed and sucked on the sweet, sweet squirtberry and didn't sleep.

A math guy on TV said, "... million hectares of frucane at eighty yield should cover four hundred million domestic mouths, plus several billion of the world's poor. It's not the farmers union, it's the math. Just doesn't add up."

"Well, Bob, you know I've been calling for an investigation of the MidWest Actuarial Corps ever since the numbers started coming out wrong. And that's easy for me to say but think about the human cost..."

Then the TV showed teeming masses of starving people, rioting, eating garbage, fighting each other all around the world, and some in the U.S. too. Men with Police or Policia or Polizia or Polis on the backs of their body armor were frying the crowds with pain guns, knocking down whole sections of them, making the hungry people squirm on the ground like they had to pee.

The girl picked up her veggie-ham mix and took a sip. And once again, the girl felt lucky.

3. DeeDee

DeeDee had no idea why she had to put up with this crap. Two snot nosed kids that should be in an Orphie, making her haul her ass out to the boondocks six days a week. She didn't understand why she wasn't on unemployment like all the other nannies. They probably hung around the local for a few hours, shooting the breeze, while she slaved away in the burbs. They probably laughed at her.

DeeDee had talked to her uncle about this travesty, because what was the use of her uncle's wife being a big party muckety muck if his family still had to work like servants? DeeDee had taken this job with the explicit understanding that *nobody used nannies anymore*, and then got hit with this bullshit.

Aunt Muckety wouldn't help. She said that the nannies union was part of the powerful Organization North - Drivers, Officers, Laborers, Etc. group (nannies, she figured, being part of the Etc.) with whom she had a cozy relationship, which she did not want messed with in any way.

But, so, then, why couldn't Muckety just put in for this one favor, DeeDee demanded? But Muck had lost interest in the conversation, and her uncle had given her a stupid robotic dog, like some kind of consolation prize.

"This is very rare, and very expensive," her uncle had said.

DeeDee had thrown it in the back of her SUV and forgotten all about it until just now, as she pulled up over the curb in front of 87823153 CloverHedge Parkway, home of the snots.

DeeDee stomped into the house carrying the dog, its fur tickling under her arm, making her drop it. The dog scrambled to a sitting position and looked up at her, tail wagging, head cocked, mouth closed and eyes bright. She ignored the dog and slouched over and unstrapped the kids, hauled them up, and flopped down into a strapchair herself.

"You didn't piss it again, did you sweetie?" DeeDee said to the girl, not too worried about it. "Put this in the TV box," she said, handing the girl a G-card. The girl took the card, stretching and taking her time, making DeeDee wait. Once the card was in, DeeDee browsed the three extra channels that you could access if you had a Level 2 card.

Garry Springer was on, and some fat people were fighting with each other about who had been sleeping with whose partner, and why, and who was still sneaking black market sodas, and how. And then it was a big fight and DeeDee got up, bored and pissed off, because she had seen this one twice and she already knew who would win the fight, and the other two channels were playing commercials.

The kids were staring, unused to anything besides the government channel. DeeDee didn't want to turn it off, because she felt uncomfortable without the noise blaring — but she didn't really want the kids watching it either. Not because she cared about it being inappropriate, or anything, but because it was *her damned G-card*.

"I got a dog right here," DeeDee said.

The kids turned, saw it, and were astonished. The girl ran over instantly and began petting its soft, silver fur. The dog opened its toothless mouth and gave her some licks with its felt tongue. The girl giggled and hopped around and clapped.

The boy sauntered over, then, and put out his hand to touch the dog but DeeDee had had enough and yelled at both of them to stop.

"That is a very expensive dog," she said, "and if you break it you know you can't be paying for it. So *back off*."

DeeDee was eating a black market Snickers as she said this, bits of chocolate and nuts and nougat showing and churning, some flecks flying out into the air. She didn't care, though, since she had a practically unlimited supply from her stupid uncle, who must have felt guilty about leaving her in this stupid job while everyone else lived the good life.

As the kids backed off from the dog, it followed them, tail wagging, mouth open and eager for play.

"Stay," said DeeDee, pointing to the corner of the room.

The dog didn't understand quickly enough, so DeeDee gave it a kick in the midsection, sending it sideways into the kitchenette table and knocking over a chair, breaking off a couple of back supports. The dog scampered to the corner, whined and hung its head, tail between its legs.

DeeDee finished her Snickers and decided to go outside for a smoke, snatching her G-card from the TV box on the way.

4. Boy

The boy edged his way along a crooked path towards the dog. The girl was alternating watching him and the TV, but the TV was some guys talking about a *dialectic*, in some kind of impossible language, so he figured she was really just watching him, and trying not to seem like it. So he hammed it up, darting glances like a thief, putting on a little show.

The dog's head was still hung, but he peered up under silvery brows, hopeful, cute, yearning. The boy reached out a tentative hand and, glancing again at the door, gave the dog's head a couple of quick pats.

The dog's silver fur felt ticklish, brilliant, alive. It raised its head and looked at him with all of the love in the universe, opened its mouth, and started licking profusely, while trying not to move its head out of the rubbing position. When the boy stopped petting for a second, the dog nuzzled his hand hard, tossing it into the air.

It was then that the boy realized that the dog could feel. He resented DeeDee for having kicked it.

The girl appeared now and was doing her share of petting, receiving her share of licks, pausing occasionally to jump up and down and issue a muted shout of glee.

"Watch the door," said the boy. "If DeeDee comes in, we'll have to scram."

"I wish Mom had a G-card like DeeDee's," said the girl, absently, still petting.

"Those channels are garbage," said the boy. "It's just as well she doesn't."

"There must be *something* good," said the girl.

The dog stopped licking, shook, and galloped over to the TV. It put its snout right up against the TV box and stuck its tongue in there, and some stuff happened and then a TV menu appeared with more selections than the kids could easily count or read.

"He understood!" shouted the girl, too loud.

"Shh!" hissed the boy, moving quickly to the TV to see what he could see. Whole categories of options had appeared, but the one that caught his eye right away was *surveillance*, because it sounded like power. He wanted to see what surveillance looked like.

The surveillance menu was endless, a labyrinth, but the boy put in their own address and then, *bam*, right there on the TV screen came a view of the backs of the two of them and the dog standing there in front of the TV. It was labeled Microcam-1.

"Woah," said the boy, then he figured out how to switch microcams to the front exterior, which he used to watch DeeDee smoking, talking on her wristphone, gesturing a lot with her cigarette hand.

For the moment, the boy felt safe.

5. Spook

Alerts were blaring *unauthorized surveillance*, so the spook threw all of the house microcam feeds up on his wallscreen. The spook's partner had been playing solitaire when his screen was replaced by a view of some lady pacing around on a curb, smoking.

"What the hell?" he said. Then, "Hey check it out, this chick has an SUV."

The spook was scanning the screens for the source of the alert, a level 7 access breach, probably the most serious offense he had ever seen. His adrenaline was up and he was jazzed to make a big play, bust someone hard, not just taxes for this one, they'd put em away.

"There," he said. But all he saw was two kids and a dog in front of a TV, watching the same microcam that he was watching, watching their own backs. Befuddled, the spook turned his attention to the dog.

"Is that one of those Swiss-Japanese jobs?" asked his partner. "An F1-D0?"

"Looks like it," said the spook, imaging the dog and sending it up for analysis. The analysis confirmed that it was an F1-D0.

"Something is wrong here," said the spook. "The microcams should have flagged the F1."

"The lady outside," said his partner.

"Right," said the spook, and he imaged her and sent it up for analysis. Imaged her truck, too, for good measure.

After a few seconds, the spook's wristphone bleeped. It was his boss's boss's boss, screaming, not listening to anything the spook had to say. The spook wanted to tell him about the access breach, and the dog, but instead he said "Yes, sir," and "I'm terribly sorry, sir." When he clicked off, he was pale.

"What the hell was that?" asked his partner.

"The girl outside is connected," said the spook. "Some of her family are party members."

"We're party members," said his partner. "Everyone is party members."

"Not the same," said the spook. "If someone imaged us and sent it up, I doubt their boss's boss would be getting reamed out as we speak."

"Shit," said his partner.

Then their boss called, apoplectic. He docked their pay, screamed and swore, and threatened to have them out on their asses if they ever so much as looked at that girl or anyone else in her family ever again.

They would get bounced from the union, and he would personally ensure that they were not eligible for unemployment.

The spook accepted this as one of the hazards of the job. He had never sent up a party member before, but he had heard of it happening, and of the consequences, and this treatment seemed pretty reasonable by comparison.

But he was still bothered by the breach, because even party members don't get that kind of access. Surveillance was reserved for the spook and his kind. He was deeply offended, and couldn't let it go.

After a few hours, the spook put the cameras back up, ignoring the protests of his partner.

And then he watched the Mom getting home, and Mom speaking heatedly to the girl, saying a nanny should arrive on time. Then the girl left, gasoline engine roaring and rubber squealing. But the dog was still there.

The spook figured it out. The dog didn't belong to the connected girl, it belonged to the Mom. And that meant, probably, so did the access breach.

The spook debated, first with himself, then with his partner, about sending up the Mom for analysis. If she was connected, they were dead. If not, then justice could be served.

"I wish there was a way to tell, before we send them up," said the spook to his partner, who nodded agreement.

Then, before he lost his nerve, he imaged the Mom and sent her up.

6. Dog

The dog was pleased when angry DeeDee left without him. He had been locked in her trunk for weeks, with nothing to do and no one to love. The dog had given himself an IQ test while he was stuck in there, because he had one handy, and what else was he going to do? So he took it, and scored 105. Not half bad, he thought. The dog really wished he could speak, but short of that, he would happily settle for some love.

The kids opened up after DeeDee left, playing and hugging and talking funny doggie talk. Even Mom got in on the action, a little. The dog recorded all of it, storing happy memories.

The kids showed Mom the new TV channels and the surveillance stuff, and Mom put her foot down. "This is not right," she said. "Someone could find out."

So the dog stuck his tongue in the TV box and undid whatever he had done, and it was done.

Mom turned off the TV and gathered the kids round for Allholiday. The dog watched, excited, but knowing his place. Two presents were extracted from a bag, not gift wrapped, but presents nonetheless.

The boy snatched his, forgetting to act cynical. It was a model of a boxcar, just like Mom's. Train hooks in front and back, so you could hook up to other boxcars and make your own greenway, if you had that kind of gold. The boy was excited, even though he would have liked a go-anywhere gasoline powered car, he said, like Nana and Grandpa used to have before they went away.

But it was a gift and it was his and he'd take it, and then he was driving it all over the floor, making the humming sound that they make, and the dog got in on the action and they were zipping it back and forth, the dog using paw and nose and trying to growl out the humming sound.

The girl got a Chris doll, perfectly androgynous, with a universally blended skin tone, sensible clothing and a pleasant sort of look. She would have liked a princess doll in pink, she said, but Mom said those had recently become illegal.

And it was a gift and it was hers and she'd take it, and then she and Chris were having tea in invisible cups, and the dog got in on the action and lapped the air out of an invisible cup of his own, sitting and wagging politely.

That night was the happiest of all their lives, they said. So they all piled into Mom's double bed, dog included, and Mom read them stories from an old, old book until all your could hear was soft breathing and the gentle thumping of the dog's tail.

In the morning there came a banging on the front door that wouldn't quit. Mom opened the door to a pair of government agents in red clip on ties and blue sport coats not really concealing their shoulder holsters.

The tall agent brushed her aside and went to examine the TV box. The regular sized agent focused on the dog, despite its attempts to hide.

"Here doggy," he said, "I won't hurt you."

Then there was crying and Mom was holding the kids, and the regular sized agent was under the kitchenette table grabbing. The dog was nipping and growling and it sounded like he was saying, "No, no no nofe! No, no no nofe!"

The agent got hold of the dog's collar and twisted, then yanked him out through wooden legs, hurting him. The dog squealed and bit the agent's arm, hard, but since he had no teeth it was probably like getting bitten by a hardcover book. But the agent let go and the dog flew to the TV, sticking its tongue into the box.

"Download video," thought the dog. "The ones who never loved me, who stole from the people, who would laugh about it in private."

And then the footage was downloaded to a secret place in the TV, and the dog left hints that he hoped the children would understand, and instructions how to invert the feed and send this footage out to the world, or at least to their local broadcast area. And then the agent had him.

The dog struggled, but in his mind he knew that he was probably making things harder on Mom and the kids. Yet he hoped that one of them would find the footage and broadcast it quickly before the agents came again, but then he felt selfish, knowing that the consequences would be severe. He stopped struggling.

Outside, the dog saw DeeDee get out of her SUV, seeing him, glaring at the agents but saying nothing. The agents kept their heads down said nothing, too.

They opened the back of the van, and the dog steeled himself for another long, lonely stay in a cage. But he saw no cage, only toothy metal rollers, flatteners, crushers. Recycling machinery. The regular sized agent fed the dog in, tail first.

The dog had known pain before. He had been beaten, had his tail and ears pulled by unruly children, even been thrown down a flight of stairs once. He was kicked by DeeDee as recently as yesterday. But he was unprepared for the feeling of being crushed between the metal rollers. By the time half of his body was through, the searing, bursting pain was overwhelming his faculties. He struggled to think one last thought, let it be a good one, before his head went through and it was all over. But all he could think of was revenge. They would find his footage and broadcast it, and he would be avenged. He clung to this thought as his neck started going through, eyes popping out with the pressure.

And then he could see no longer, and therefore he could not see the tall agent holding the TV box out towards the rollers, making ready to feed it in after him.

Mr. Jones *works in the fields of a tobacco plantation in Cuba. Despite being ridiculously old, he recently learned English from a Guantanamo escapee, which skill he used to scrawl out this short story on discarded leaves. He may have also written a novel recently, but unless it gets published somehow that information is about as good as idle speculation. Mr. Jones's blog can be found at* tobaccojones.com.

GROUP *by Luke Spooner*

Luke Spooner *a.k.a. 'Carrion House' currently lives and works in the South of England. Having recently graduated from the University of Portsmouth with a first class degree he is now a full time illustrator for just about any project that peaks his interest. Despite regular forays into children's books and fairy tales his true love lies in anything macabre, melancholy or dark in nature and essence. He believes that the job of putting someone else's words into a visual form, to accompany and support their text, is a massive responsibility as well as being something he truly treasures.*

www.carrionhouse.com
www.facebook.com/carrionhouse

The House

Carol Hornak

The jar of spaghetti sauce moved toward the edge and fell
onto the floor.
Splattering.
As the house hadn't gotten over its last heartbreak.

Four walls are stripped; harsh love leaves the house feeling
raw and exposed.
The sanding, with final conclusion of painting,
Then to the hands of a child pat-pat-patting a rhythm to spa-
ghetti tossed at its walls.
To a resultant scrubbing,

The woman gripping the wall in an embrace.
If only the house hadn't experienced such jubilant joy with
this. 'Cause it had wanted—heck no, desired—this person as
its own.
Had thought she would become part of its walls; at least the
musky vanilla-bean perfume might cover up that of mildew
along seams in the bathroom and resulting from past tenants
but kept active by dampness the house couldn't hold back-
—its tears.

As once wet, dripping, sloppy and emasculating umbrellas
were flung
And reconciliatory passages hurtled across its rooms
The woman left.

The person now examining it for possible future residence was spraying its rooms with lavender perfume and, again, leaving.

Venturing forth through a fog of uncertainty, the house moved beyond the survival mode. As a new potential victim was walking through.

Carol Hornak *lives in suburban New Jersey with her husband and has three children. A former preschool teacher, she currently writes poetry, short stories and is working on a novel. She has had stories published in* Liquid Imagination, Black Fox Literary Magazine *and on the website of* Abandoned Towers; *poems in* The Battered Suitcase *and* The Ranfurly Review.

THE LAST PROMISE *by Denny E. Marshall*

Denny E Marshall *has had art, poetry and fiction published, some recently.
He is just an average person. He does not know any famous.*

Blood Debt

JD Cano

The days had long since grown shorter in length and the air cooler in temperature so it held no surprise that I could see breath passing my lips. I concentrated and stared at each wisp of escaping heat, trying to determine at what point it ceased to exist outside my body. In my chest I felt the beating of my heart and tried to sense the warmth of the sun fragment in it. My fire still burned. A fervent uproar of shouts poured forth from the thousands surrounding the Templo Mayor to the sight of a lifeless body rolling down the steps towards them, bringing me out of my contemplation. My bindings tightened as the rope joining us pulled, bringing me one cold step closer to the top of the temple.

The body landed on a growing pile of broken flesh at the base of the temple, splattering blood on the worshippers front most of the crowd. Classes intermingled together, pressed together tightly from the base of the temple across the flats to the other structures. The last of the festivities seemed to have brought all the population of Tenochtitlan out to watch the blood offerings.

"It is a great honor to be sacrificed to Huitzilopochtli and pay my blood debt," I quietly said to myself.

My new position brought the priests into view, one for each corner of the large stone slab awaiting its new arrival. A fifth priest with blood stained hands signaled to the guards for the next prisoner, number twelve of the sixty to be offered before the bloodthirsty god of war that day. This month of Panquetzaliztli belonged to Huitzilopochtli, god of war and sun. After weeks of races and feasts, the sacrifices marked the end of celebration and the beginning of the repayment of the blood borrowed from the gods.

A feathered Aztec warrior cut an elderly beggar from the rope, his body containing signs of recent imprisonment. As the Eagle led him forward, the man turned to run. Barely more than a skeleton with skin, the warrior brought down the pitiful dirty man with ease. Armed with a flint knife, the Eagle made quick work of the beggar's heels, ending his wandering intents.

Kicking and screaming, the beggar was dragged to the table leaving a twin set of scarlet pools behind. The Eagle Warrior lifted the man up and threw him onto the altar easily. I had once seen my youngest daughter in a fit of rage toss her straw stuffed doll about with just as much ease, but unlike her doll, the beggar yelled in protest. His sweat mixed with a stream of tears and burrowed trails of cleanliness down his face. With his remaining energy the beggar struggled and cursed against the priests that now held him down, arching his back to the sky in a desperate attempt to free himself. I felt shame that I would soon follow such a pitiful example of a man as a fellow god-dead.

The high priest nodded to the others who each pulled tightly at one of the man's limbs out and down, flattening him against the stone. He screamed in pain and began a chain of incoherent babbling with only the occasional words of "please" and "freedom" understood. I looked towards the unmoved faces of the high nobility who chose to share their presence, seated in their gold and stone decorated chairs of luxury. As I did, one of the male members of the court glanced back at me. I silently nodded, sending my thoughts that I would die better. He remained stone faced.

I looked back to the offering place to see the priest holding his tecpatlixquahua high in the air, the sun making the polished obsidian gleam. He spoke prayers to the god of war, honoring him in his month, and brought the knife down into the beggar's abdomen. A final exhale of steam and suffering streamed forth from him. As the priest ripped out and held his still beating heart to the sun, the beggar's head dropped to the side and stared blankly at me. He blinked once, twice, and then closed them forever.

I have killed men before. I have captured them and offered them up for sacrifice and slavery. But I have never stared in their eyes at that moment when their blood and heat were returned to the gods and they died with a finality that ended everything they were. Thoughts of how I had gotten here and what I left behind entered my mind.

Along with my fellow warriors of Tlaxcala, we had dotted the ridge line like so many agave plants when the Aztec warriors arrived; their Eagles and Jaguars mixed amongst the lower warrior classes who wished to capture enough men to move up in rank. Armed with our cuauholli, our clubs, we stood ready to take or be taken. I had always fared well in the flower wars in that I always managed to come home, but this xochiyaoyotl would be my last either way. The dusk of my warrior days had come; my aging body now better suited to farming maize and feeding my five children than facing the might of the Aztec nation. Now it seemed, I would feed the gods instead, leaving my family to find their own path.

Once again the rope tightened pulling me up one more step to my end and I muttered to myself, "I shall be sacrificed to Huitzilopochtli."

Ahuiliztli, a fellow warrior of my village, stood as the only man in front of me awaiting his turn. Like me, he presented himself before the crowd stripped of his warrior garb apart from his head dressings. We wore meager cloth garments which would have normally suited me; however, this day seemed to grow colder instead of warmer which caused my skin to ache. I expected to see Ahuiliztli standing proud and ready, but when I looked to him, there loomed only an empty shell of the warrior I knew and the day grew colder still.

As the Eagle Warrior cut him from the rope and walked him towards the slab, Ahuiliztli called upon his last bit of courage and walked with little guidance and with no struggle. I could see only the slightest of trembling as one of the priests removed his over garment, leaving him only in a waist wrapping. Upon seeing the warrior head-dress of the next sacrifice the crowd surrounding the temple rose to a new level of hysteria. I looked down to see women, men and children raising hands, screaming to the heavens. A group of them kneeled before the temple, crowded by the freshly hollowed out dead bodies, cutting slits into their ears with knifes or puncturing their skin with thorns in personal offerings of their own blood. Even the paper flags adorning the buildings behind them fluttered more violently in the wake of the kill to come.

Just three days before, I had been by Ahuiliztli's side awaiting the coming of the battle. Friends since childhood, there remained little of the man that I did not know. Our children often played together and on a few occasions I was friend enough to quickly hide him away after he had drunk too much octli in the night. His opinion of the xochiyaoyotl dwindled as he advanced in years but he and I both kept his pessimistic views to ourselves.

"They tell us lies, Toltecatl", he told me. "These wars serve no purpose that benefit our people."

I looked over my shoulder to him and asked in a mocking manner, "Is that so, my friend?"

"Do not act like you do not know, or have at least never thought so. What do we do here? They are not invading; they are not destroying or even killing. We stand here and we fight to trade blows and take prisoners. Like children playing a game. And for every prisoner we take they take four or more. So while the large empire of the Aztec gets scratched, the Tlaxcala bleeds at the throat."

"So tell me then, Ahuiliztli, why do you come to fight?"

"I stand here, Toltecatl, so no one else must, and because others still believe."

Now my friend lay on the table, continuing to do his part to fill the blood thirst of the gods. He clenched his teeth together to hold back his screams, but when the priest brought down his blade, driving it deep into my friend, he gasped out in a rage. Like the beggar before him, I watched Ahuiliztli let his life escape with one final exhale of white breath.

While the high priest offered up his heart to the sun, another priest took the time to cut off Ahuiliztli's head. Upon placing the still decorated head on a spike of the temple's highest step the crowd's roar broke into a feverish pitch like utter lunacy. They seemed just as blood thirsty as the god of war himself. A Jaguar Warrior emerged up from the back steps of the temple to receive the body of my now dead friend. He would take it home, this body he had captured, and after dividing it up would gift each piece out for a tiny feast. Such was the way. The rope tightened, pulling me to the sacrifice plateau, and the realization that my turn now arrived washed over me with a final wave of cold.

"I shall be sacrificed," I mumbled to myself.

"What was that you said, teo micqui?"

I looked at the speaker and for the first time noticed the face beneath the Eagle Warrior headset. The last time I saw this face it grimaced as it bore down a sword, broadside, against my head. Only a momentary flash of anger fought to overtake me as I stared into the eyes of my captor; just a brief second of pondering the possibility of taking his knife, opening his throat and making upon my escape. It passed as I felt I could not begrudge someone who merely chose to exist as another believer.

When I did not answer, the warrior merely shrugged off the interaction. Perhaps he thought I spoke a quiet prayer or let slip a curse, both which he would continue to hear in abundance. Cutting me free from the group rope, he walked me by my bindings to the table. Knowing me as a warrior he remained tense, hand on the hilt of his weapon, looking for any possible signs of struggle. He need not worry; a trance overtook me as I slid my feet along the short distance to my end. No danger of him losing his prize existed. It startled me to see that my hands shook as the bindings came off. I did not feel it. My sight dropped to the people as my top was removed. I observed the same open mouthed, screaming fanatics as before, but did not hear them. The coldness finally succeeded in numbing me and spread to all my external senses.

Falling back I landed upon the slab. I felt as if I should fall more, further and further down into a deep sanctuary of my own design, but the altar of the gods and the zealots stopped me. Memories of my family now came to me. I thought of my wife, Necahual, and how she would have to look after our children and learn to live on her own strength. I wondered if she thanked the gods for my chance to give of myself as a god-dead sacrifice. My eldest son would help her, but would soon come of age to possibly join the flower wars and seek vengeance. Life would continue and follow full circle for the believers.

As I lay, I looked into the sun high above, feeling my own heart beat within me for a few moments more. The priest now stood over me, knife high and ready. I let out one final deep breath and saw that it carried no tendrils of a smoky spirit.

"I shall be killed."

JD Cano *is a part time writer, full time story creator. He currently lives in Texas with his fiance, their son and two dogs. He enjoys hikes and the outdoors when it isn't blistering hot, and catching up on the television stories when it is. Keep up with him at* http://www.facebook.com/JDCanoWrites *or follow him at @jd_Cano.*

Subscribe to

BÊTE NOIRE

1 year, 4 issues
$23.95*

Send email to: subscribe @betenoiremagazine.com

Or fill out the form below and send, along with check or
money order made payable to Jennifer Gifford to:

P.O. Box 1545
Highland, MI 48357

Name:_____

Address: _____

Email:_____

Susbcription includes Dark Opus Press's annual anthology

*US and Canada only, international subscriptions $29.95/year